Rhinos for Lunch and Elephants for Supper!

A Maasai Tale By
TOLOLWA M. MOLLEL

Illustrated by
BARBARA SPURLL

Clarion Books
New York

To Uju
– T. M. M.

To my husband
– B. S.

Clarion Books
a Houghton Mifflin Company imprint
215 Park Avenue South, New York, NY 10003
Text copyright © 1991 by Tololwa M. Mollel
Illustrations copyright © 1991 by Barbara Spurll
First published in Canada by Oxford University Press Canada,
70 Wynford Drive, Don Mills, Ontario, M3C 1J9

For information about permission to reproduce selections from this
book, write to Permissions, Houghton Mifflin Company,
215 Park Avenue South, New York, NY 10003.

Printed in Hong Kong.

Library of Congress Cataloging-in-Publication Data

Mollel, Tololwa M. (Tololwa Marti)
Rhinos for lunch and elephants for supper! / by Tololwa M. Mollel
illustrated by Barbara Spurll.
p.   cm.
Summary: A variety of animals try to help a hare get rid of the
mysterious intruder who has taken over her house.
ISBN 0-395-60734-5 PA ISBN 0-618-05156-2
[1. Folklore, Masai. 2. Animals—Folklore.] I. Spurll, Barbara, ill.
II. Title.
PZ8.1.M73Rh 1991   91-19365
398.2—dc20   CIP
[E]   AC

SCO 10 9 8 7

After a pleasant walk in the forest, a little hare cheerfully arrived back at the cave where her den was hidden.

"I'll hop in," she thought happily,
"roast a few nuts for lunch,
and have a peaceful nap."

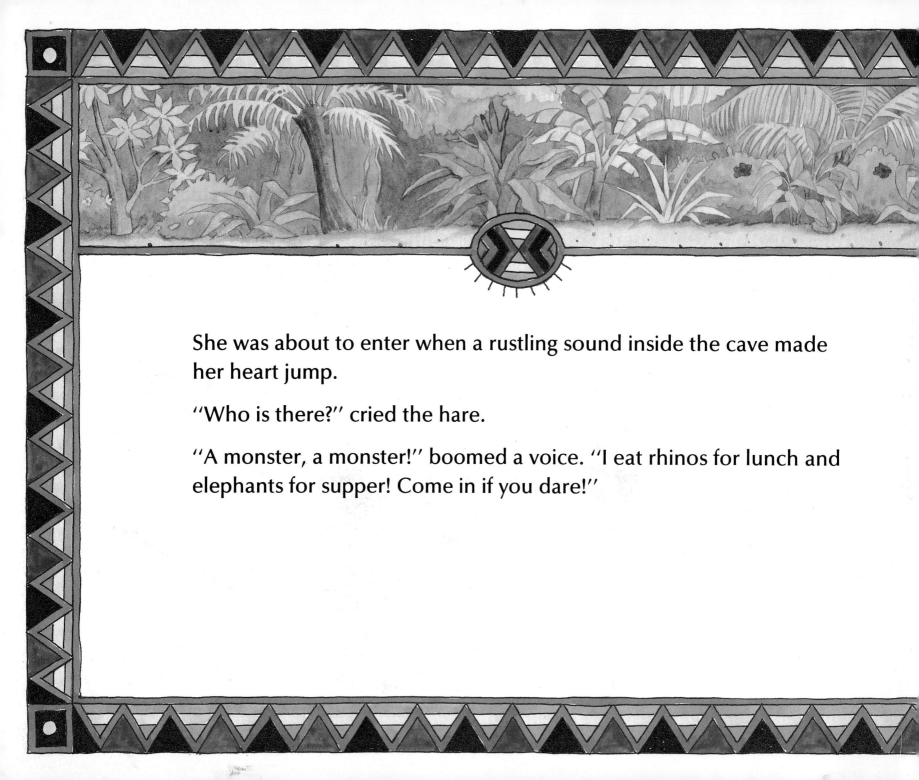

She was about to enter when a rustling sound inside the cave made her heart jump.

"Who is there?" cried the hare.

"A monster, a monster!" boomed a voice. "I eat rhinos for lunch and elephants for supper! Come in if you dare!"

The hare was terrified and ran away.

Along the way, she met a fox and told him of the monster. "I'll get him out for you!" said the fox.

"You can't!" shrieked the hare. "He eats rhinos for lunch and elephants for supper!"

"Come, I'll sink my teeth into him and drive him away!" the fox boasted.

At the cave, the fox bared his teeth and barked, "This is the home of my friend the hare. Come out, you bully of a monster, before I sink my teeth into your neck!"

"I'm a monster, a monster!" came the voice, rocking the earth and echoing through the forest. "I eat rhinos for lunch and elephants for supper! Come in if you dare!"

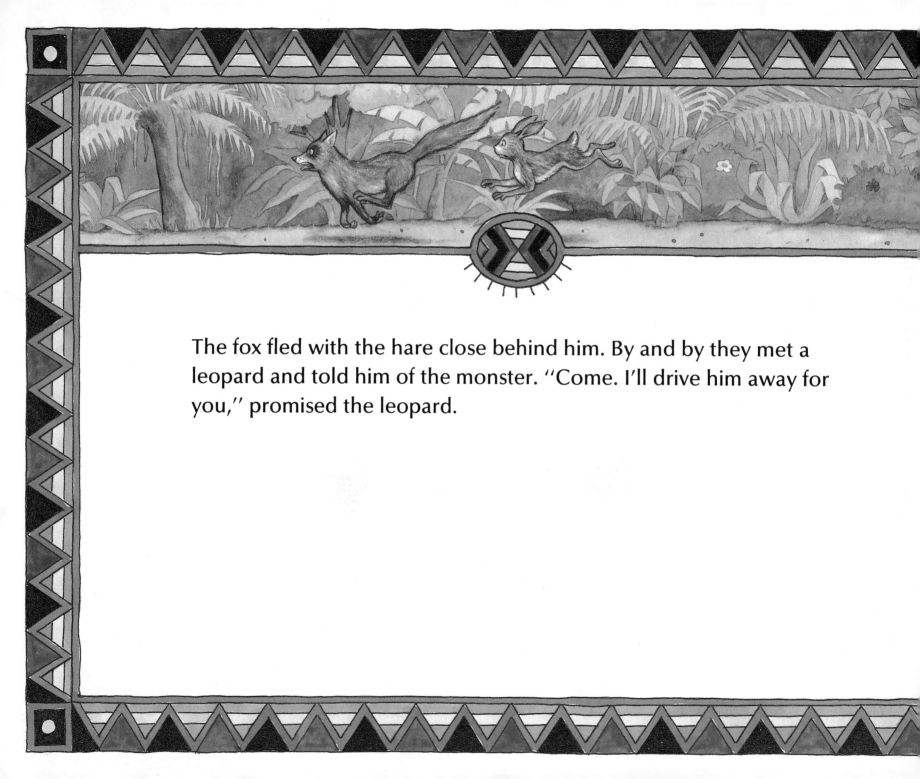

The fox fled with the hare close behind him. By and by they met a leopard and told him of the monster. "Come. I'll drive him away for you," promised the leopard.

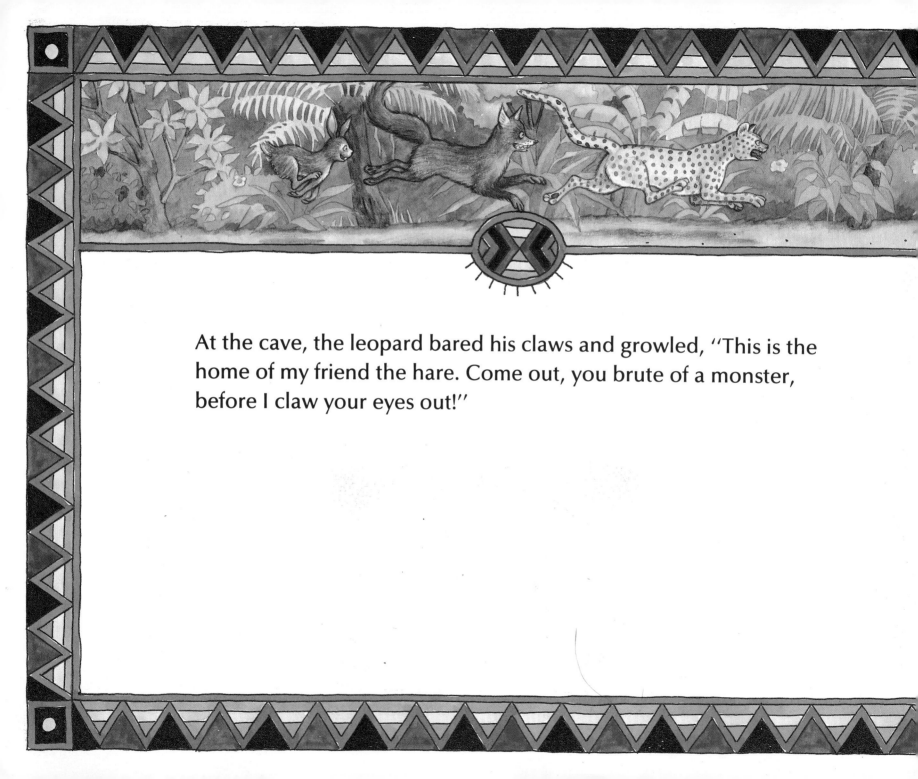

At the cave, the leopard bared his claws and growled, "This is the home of my friend the hare. Come out, you brute of a monster, before I claw your eyes out!"

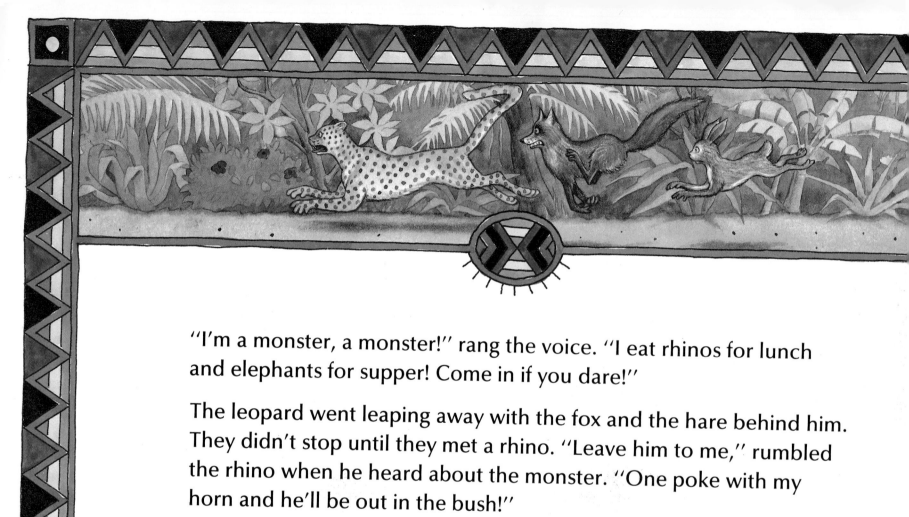

"I'm a monster, a monster!" rang the voice. "I eat rhinos for lunch and elephants for supper! Come in if you dare!"

The leopard went leaping away with the fox and the hare behind him. They didn't stop until they met a rhino. "Leave him to me," rumbled the rhino when he heard about the monster. "One poke with my horn and he'll be out in the bush!"

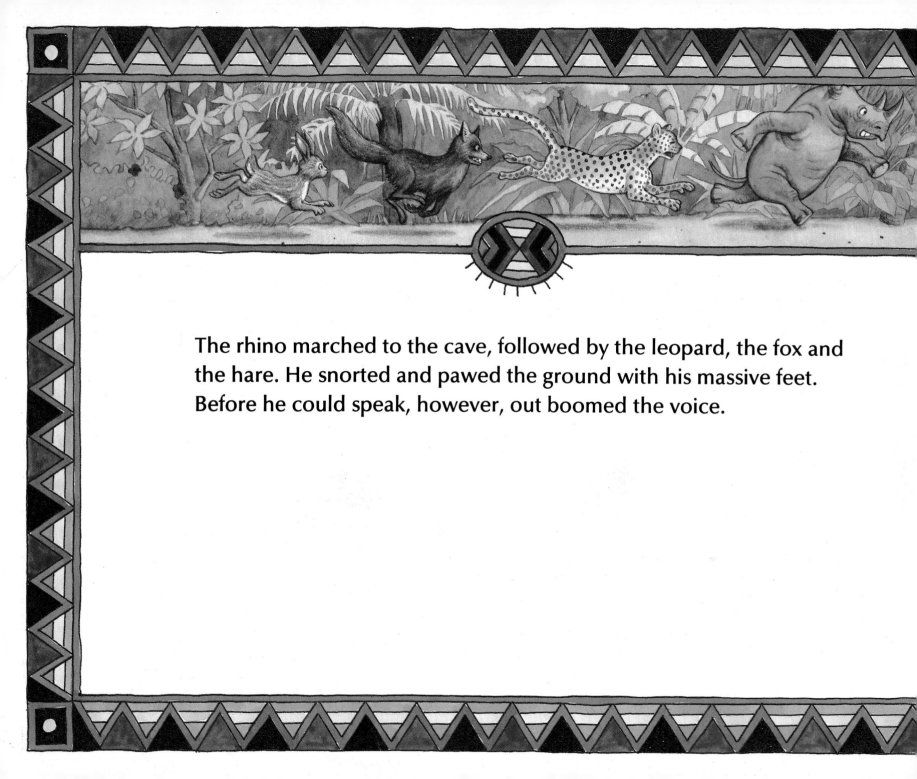

The rhino marched to the cave, followed by the leopard, the fox and the hare. He snorted and pawed the ground with his massive feet. Before he could speak, however, out boomed the voice.

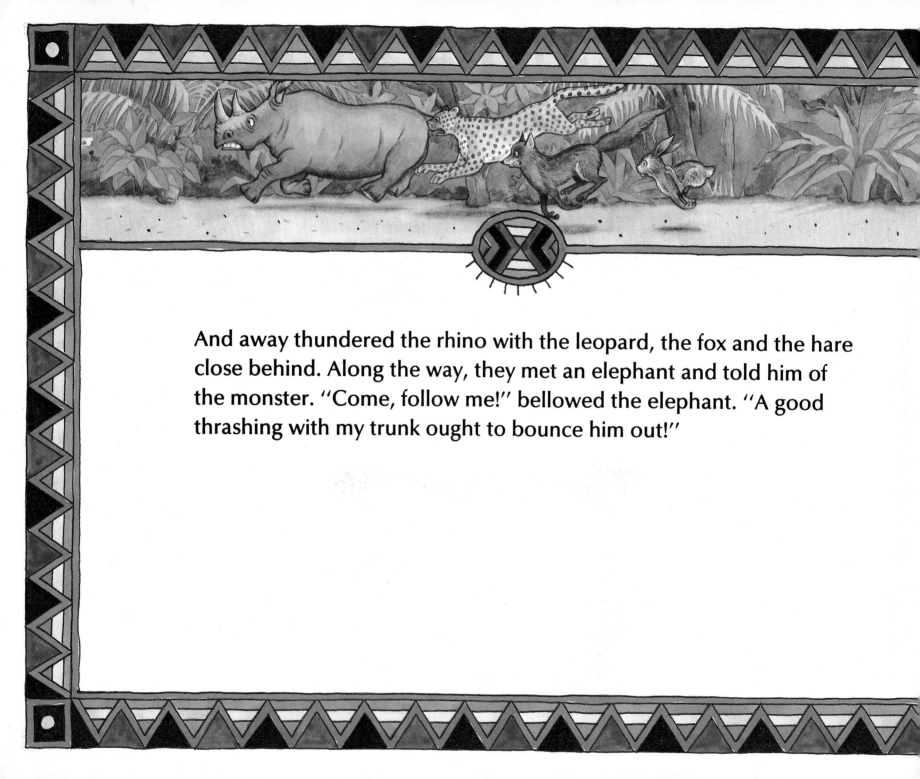

And away thundered the rhino with the leopard, the fox and the hare close behind. Along the way, they met an elephant and told him of the monster. "Come, follow me!" bellowed the elephant. "A good thrashing with my trunk ought to bounce him out!"

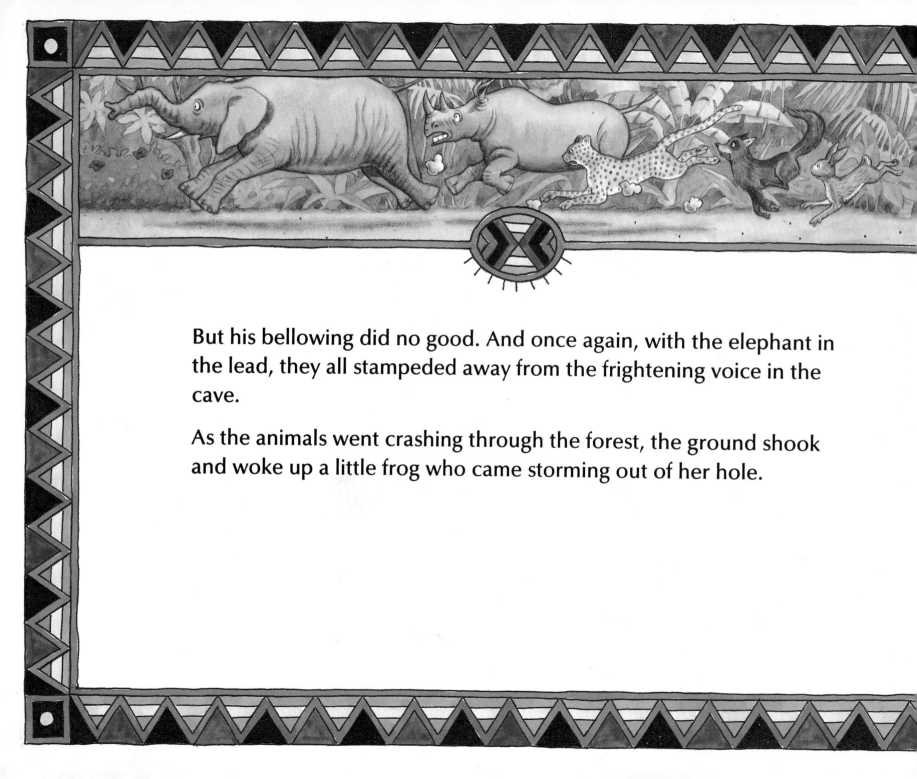

But his bellowing did no good. And once again, with the elephant in the lead, they all stampeded away from the frightening voice in the cave.

As the animals went crashing through the forest, the ground shook and woke up a little frog who came storming out of her hole.

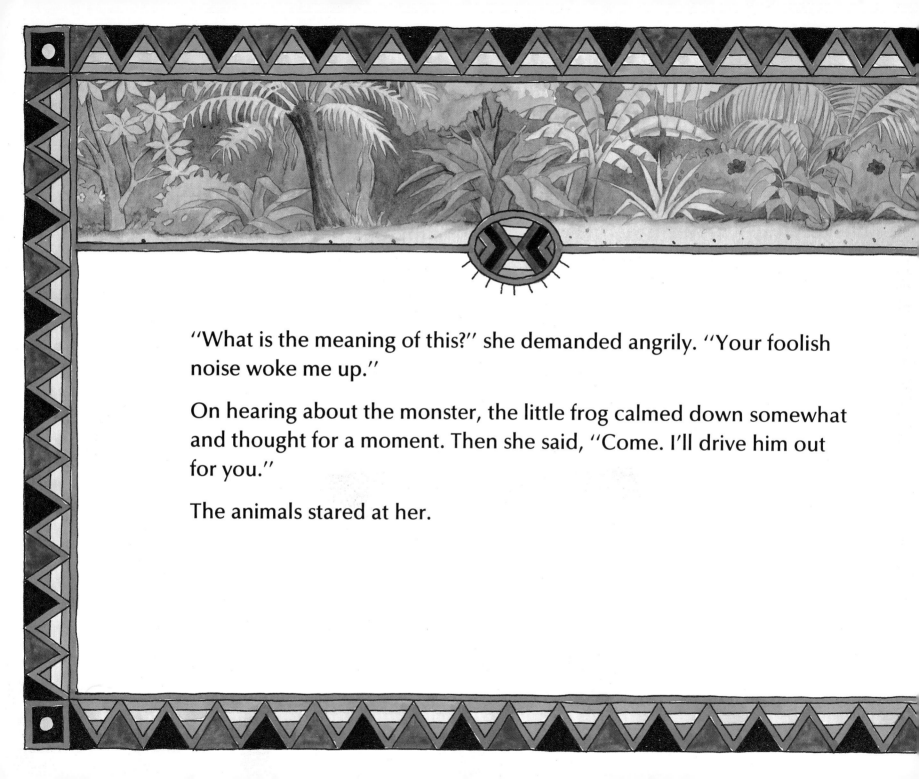

"What is the meaning of this?" she demanded angrily. "Your foolish noise woke me up."

On hearing about the monster, the little frog calmed down somewhat and thought for a moment. Then she said, "Come. I'll drive him out for you."

The animals stared at her.

"You . . ."

"a frog . . ."

"will drive out the monster . . ."

"who eats rhinos for lunch . . ."

"and elephants for supper?!"

"If I'm to finish my nap I'll have to," sighed the frog. Then chewing on her pipe and swinging her walking stick, she led the way, cool and confident as can be.

When she got to the cave, she said to the monster, "This is the home of my great friend the hare. Come out, whoever you are, before I come in and get you."

"I'm a monster, a monster!" came the reply. "I eat rhinos for lunch and elephants for supper! Come in if you dare."

"I'm the great eater, the great eater," boomed back the frog. "I eat rhinos for breakfast, elephants for lunch and *monsters for supper*! I'm coming, I'm coming!"

Everything was silent. Then out of the dark crawled a tiny caterpillar, blinking his eyes and rubbing his ears. "My word," he exclaimed in a small voice, "what an echo there is in this cave! Hardly the place to stay for a snooze." And to himself he added, "Though I did try my best!" With a mischievous wink, he merrily sauntered on his way.

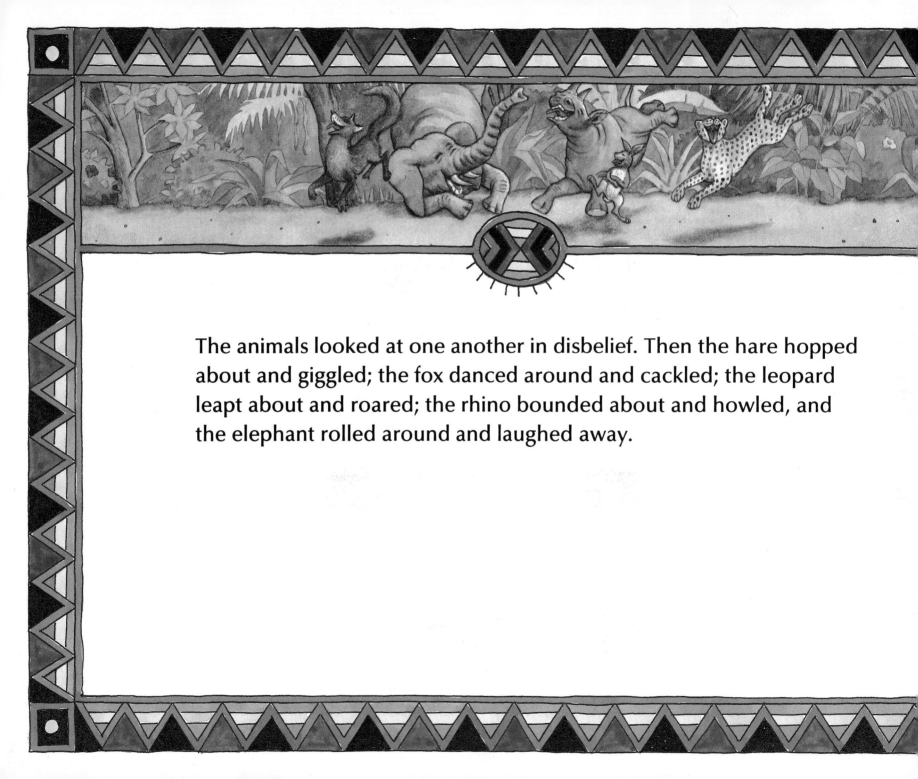

The animals looked at one another in disbelief. Then the hare hopped about and giggled; the fox danced around and cackled; the leopard leapt about and roared; the rhino bounded about and howled, and the elephant rolled around and laughed away.

As for the brave little frog, she didn't so much as crack a smile. "Come with me," she called after the caterpillar. "I know just the place for . . ." she turned and glowered at the laughing animals, "an *un*interrupted afternoon nap."

Then, swinging her walking stick and chewing on her pipe, she led the way, cool and confident as can be.